'Dangerously addictive.'
The Guardian

'Harwicz succeeds in luring the reader into the darker
aspects of the human mind.'
Publisher's Weekly

'Uncomfortable and fascinating, Harwicz drags us on a turbulent
voyage of self-discovery.'
Vanity Fair

'Harwicz is an intensely passionate and fearless writer whose
irresistible prose deserves to be read far and wide.'
Claire-Louise Bennet, author of CHECKOUT 19

'Unrelenting and unforgettable, Harwicz is one of the most
formidable writers at work today.'
Jeremy Garber, *Powell's*

'We are used to female narrators who occupy one of several familiar
niches (...). Harwicz takes us somewhere more profound and forces
us to confront the thought that these easy fictional "explanations"
are specious. Lurking inside all of us is the potential for horror.'
Hari Kunzru, author of RED PILL

'The acoustic quality of her prose, the pulse of her voice, the
intensity of her imagery make her subjects so daring, so relentless, so
damned and unconventional – very hard to drop or ever to forget.'
Lina Meruane, author of NERVOUS SYSTEM

TENDER

First published by Charco Press 2022
Charco Press Ltd., Office 59, 44-46 Morningside Road,
Edinburgh, EH10 4BF

Copyright © Ariana Harwicz 2015
First published in Spanish as *Precoz* by Mardulce (Argentina)
English translation copyright © Annie McDermott & Carolina Orloff 2022

Work published with funding from the 'Sur' Translation Support Programme
of the Ministry of Foreign Affairs of Argentina / Obra editada en el marco
del Programa 'Sur' de Apoyo a las Traducciones del Ministerio de Relaciones
Exteriores y Culto de la República Argentina.

A CIP catalogue record for this book is available from the British Library.

ISBN: 9781913867126
e-book: 9781913867133

www.charcopress.com

Edited & proofread by Fionn Petch
Cover designed by Pablo Font
Typeset by Laura Jones

Ariana Harwicz

TENDER

Translated by
Annie McDermott & Carolina Orloff

I wake up gaping like a force-fed duck when they strip its liver out to make foie gras. My body is here, my mind over there and outside something thuds like a dry heave. It's dark still and two birds flap violently out of my tree, collide in mid-air and fall dead. I look to see if he's written. One eye open all night long, checking in my sleep. The fire pulls. I threw on a couple of damp, hollow logs and stuck my head halfway up the chimney till they caught. The room filled with smoke. Mum and Dad's photo on the hearth. I was dreaming, am dreaming, of lupins, stems of flowers blooming white, pink and lilac, then the pods and seeds begin to form. I woke up. A sound on the stairs, four legs in freefall land in my lap. I sit and doze facing the boarded-up window with my hand laid over the cat. The child comes tumbling down the stairs. Bloody-kneed, calling for me. Mum. Mum. I'm awake in the rocking chair right by the banister but I keep my eyes tight shut. The fire no longer there. I have to get something to rub on his knees, I have to comfort him but I can't move. The image of a young woman like white cows pushing at the wood-panelled window, desperate to spear her way in. A boar-woman flattening the fence, ready to trample me, that stranger who has me up against the bars. Where's the surgical spirit asks the boy, where's the surgical spirit madame ask the illegal workers peering out of their booths, look, lady, he's bleeding on the stones. I find the bottle, clean the wound and put my arms around my son. But he's grown too big, too long, he's outstripping me. As I climb the stairs, his feet dangle and swing and I drop him not far from the top. You're too heavy now, you great big lump, his body doubling mine. When he turns away to get dressed I look down at the bright pure specks on the white stones. Then we climb into the mangled car and off I go, the needle jumping to the top and the speed making him sick. The lycée door locked, we pound with our fists and scream our heads off like a couple of misfits. The caretaker glares through the glass, she's used to us now, then lets us in and he disappears down the corridors. I swear he always sneaks straight out the other side.

Impossible to describe a whole day in his arms, heavy artillery fire amid roars of laughter and tortured venison pâté. Halcyon days. A woodland picnic in fancy dress, him in shorts and braces, me in a smock stamped with smeary hydrangeas. An afternoon with the crossbow, the catapult, smoking and half-litre bottles. Lighting cigars and snuffing them out when our mouths are musty sculptures. An afternoon in convoy to the local fair, to try our luck on the Gypsies' rusty slot machines, then trying again, tipping in whole tubs of coins until the prizes come cascading out and we jump up and down among the caravans. From the glass case full of garish tags, we pick a laser gun. And then we scribble all over the river, with the laser between our legs we write our names in capitals and wrap them in a heart, just like the one he draws in sperm on my face. Or all over the flying centipede where couples drool on each other, sheltered by the canopy as they clatter round the bend. A salty kiss with tongues and chewing gum just before the jolt. A liquid kiss in the gap of the lips. We'll go to the sea one day he says and it's enough for me, to the sea one day. An impossible kiss. Back to the mental age when the world was all wide-open craggy heights. The mental age of questions. Why do the Alps make you want to die. Why can't the heart keep still and why isn't the brain smooth to the touch. The mental age of unwholesome love.

Why is ogling each other so terrifying, back to the pure age of my only son. What's it like being old, Mum? When I grow up you'll be deader than dead, by the time I'm a father you won't be a mother, don't get upset, and he laughs. The two of us stare at the motorway, imagine spilling oil by the gallon then getting out of the way to watch the cars skid, spin like turnstiles and capsize.

I know he left at the end of the afternoon and I waved goodbye through the window, smiled in the rear-view mirror, my lips discoloured and his silk scarf wrapped around my head. I know I went to pick my son up from school and he came out embarrassed in front of his classmates and slunk into the back seat. I look at how I'm dressed. I don't see the problem. And he requested upbeat music and on the suspension bridge over the sandbanks asked me what we were doing that weekend. But I just drove to the supermarket. We filled the trolley with tins, ant poison, cold meats and ran down the aisles, pocketing batteries and disposable razors, sometimes switching things around on the shelves. All smiles and lovey-dovey whispers together at the checkout and then I pay, we take the bags and head for the exit as usual. Him whistling a ballad and me gazing out at the clouds strangling the sky. The line of trolleys moving by itself between the dented cars when a man shows us his badge and asks us to follow him. The minor and me in the basement, stacks of boxes everywhere, wads of banknotes counted by gloved hands and security guards. Excuse me, what's that in your pockets? Razors and batteries fall to the floor. How old is the boy? Is he your son? Is he in school? We have some questions for him, routine stuff, and he's led away and surrounded by women in pencil skirts. But it's only me he looks at. It's only me he loves. A caution from the local police, next up a visit from social services and a criminal record. And nothing for us to shave with.

On the way home, darting over the tarmac ahead we see a rabbit with blue eyes. We honk the horn, shout through the windows. My son reaches right out and the wind helps him stroke her but she's running too fast, never straying off the road. We splash her with water but she won't go into the trees, she won't be drawn by the forest. We see her bounding, flying, soaring before us. We watch her take on the cars and escape unscathed, defying the law of the jungle. Then we cross the estuary fields and the sound of a swan's beating heart is so intense that it makes us cry.

At the weekend we decamp to the lounge and the frozen garden. I play ping-pong on a table he assembled and painted but I can't coordinate my hand movements and my son swears at me every time I serve. You need glasses, you need a girdle, you need more practice. My little ray of sunshine. We stop for a snack, chocolate milk with a drizzle of port, oatmeal biscuits and the hours edge by like a string of executions. With each rifle drill, the terror returns. My son dozes off, stretched long in my lap, his arm over my bare legs, my shawl, the weight of his head my first indication that he's become a man. I dream of a sailing boat, him and me taking turns at the rudder. One of us down below opening the tin of sardines, changing the oil, polishing the tools. Both wearing turbans. And the day comes when I look at him and love him so much that I say wait for me on deck with your eyes shut. Then I reach under the bed for the sackcloth bag, the surprise, the gun and I shoot him.

It's a shock waking up on a Saturday night and finding my son on top of me. Where are the other kids your age, what do they do, what makes kids your age laugh, where do they go, do they queue outside the nightclub with the wooden floor and mirror balls, do they fiddle with themselves behind the hill. How do they talk, what do they wear, what cigarettes do they smoke. Have the breakouts started, the wet dreams, are they allowed mopeds, what time do their progenitors expect them home. At the front door, his car with the see-through roof, full beams on the shrews as they nibble each other and I push him off. He folds into the chair. I get up with cramp but when I step outside the car surges away from the farm. Inside me everything darkens until the pines are swishing like whips.

I think of the men buried yards from their enemy. I think of the survivors who fraternised the next Christmas. That unreal 1915 night when they all sat around the table with steaming plates, their fists dripping onto the cutlery. Those men who lived in caves for months and years come bearing down on me. I wonder how they managed to jerk off in the mud, in the water, amid crippled corpses, limbless bodies, among spilling guts, pools of blood and lice-infested sinks. How they managed when the moon shone orange on their paths to drink their piss down to the dregs. I'd have made sure to get myself killed on day one.

The weekend is not easily disposed of. We drag ourselves out for a walk. No one reports things any more, after all it took years to persuade the police about Vita the painter, that she'd never stop exhuming dead animals and each arrest cost the community in taxes. Before, officers would turn up at all hours, cart her off to give a statement, seize sacks full of bones and struggling animals they never knew what to do with. And when piles formed on the road to the village or in the scrapheaps nearby, the neighbours would be straight back on the phones, curtains twitching in the dead of night. Her house, the smallest, built on the bones of the last, was also full of foetuses in jars. She spent whole days shut away in there, mainlining morphine, painting the decomposing colours of the fish she picked up at the port. Whole days under the influence, demolishing herself. My son looks around, the earth sealed over. No more calls to the police, the ground smooth beneath the weight of the fruit trees, no more scattered bones, no one opening tombs or bringing creepy crawlies to the table. We get a wave from a young Czech on a step with a hip flask, in army trousers and a red polo shirt. One foot raised like he's training for the army, and a brush in his hand dipped in white paint. Vita ventures out behind him, obese in her pregnancy, smiling like she's bound for the electric chair. We wave at her and watch as she carries out her jars, making the most of her Sunday. Clean and tidy, clean and tidy, shouts the Czech with his thick accent, his tongue pressed flat behind his teeth. Order over chaos, he yells enraptured at a leader. And off we go, the house white and empty in our wake. The neighbours want to canonise the Czech because he made her stop painting. No one to play against or box in these parts, he makes balls of frost and sludge and lobs them over the pediment with pro-Russian zeal. I slink away when no one's looking, take the narrow, razed path alongside the house, pull up nettles and eat them as I go. The son doesn't make me happy, the son doesn't fill me. I feel like a hair in a bottle of alcohol, adrift alive and dead. Madame could be a grandma by now, when's it to be they ask at the market among the olives, fried food and local goats' cheese. I carry on walking, try to slip between the stalls, when's it to be, my contorted neck. An erection, I need to achieve an erection and I cut loose from my surroundings, I'm not where I'm treading, not madame in the hat, the teenage boy's keeper, not hacking my way through the underbrush. The other people in heat are no help. Quick. Anything will do. An erection to keep me going. An erection as the instinct to resist, an erection so I can stay on my feet and play boules with the others and make dinner. Something to rise up from the weeds and dry moss. An erection to get me through, through the Sunday, through the chores, through the chitchat, the alleged love of grandchildren. Now I see, tall bright pines and their shadows flicker like ill-buried youths under vaulted roofs, like misspelt conscripts on memorial slabs, like unrecorded First World War soldiers. I'd go out tonight and collect the ashes of everyone shot by a firing squad or beheaded in the desert. When I got back he was dehydrated on the table like an upside-down fishbowl. Wakey wakey, let's do some boxing, I shove at his shoulder but he doesn't react. He has sideburns now, ear hair, his armpits reek of the sporting elite or the builders over the road. BO already; my mutant son. I kick him, shake him by the pyjama shirt, his first instinct to pounce and attack but when he sees me he holds off. He's still half-asleep when I put him in the car, no seatbelt and away we go for the first time all weekend. I accelerate so hard we smell the engine burning, I mess up the gears, my foot strimming the clutch. No one anywhere in these parts late on a Sunday, not abseiling down the walls of the game preserve or smuggling bell jars into the catacombs. No one on the viaduct walking the train tracks like a tightrope, flanked by thirty-thousand-volt cables. We watch the sky as it spreads like smoke past the family wineries and breweries with grain sacks outside, then slow down and unscrew a bottle with our teeth.

The next morning I'm not doing so well sprawled on the floor at the foot of his bed. We split the room in two with plasterboard a while back and now we don't see each other naked or under the covers, and he doesn't reach giggling for my tits. The alarm goes off and nothing in the house is ready. The first thing I see in the lounge is an overturned glass and water pooling on the wood. The glass was full when we went to bed, the cat's outside, this house makes no sense. There's nothing for breakfast, hordes of ants and blowflies have eaten the leftovers. Sorry I say, sorry, I forgot to cover the bread. Don't go to school today. Stay here with me, I'm sorry, I'll take you tomorrow and just then I see a short woman walking along and looking in our direction. Come on, don't be so selfish, you won't miss much today and I need you, what could they possibly learn. And a hand is ringing our bell. Who's that, my son out of the nest. No idea, just ignore it. And he gets dressed because of me. The ringing again. How are we meant to get out with her in the way, she's not leaving, not moving, must be here to sell something, then she reaches through the railings and lets herself in. What a nerve. Who is it he says, brushing his teeth. No idea. Our only option to confront her. I open the shutters, my voice faint. Yes? Good morning, I'm here from social services, I'd like a word if possible since I've come all this way. I had such a palaver finding the house, there's no street name, no number. Sitting opposite me she heard noises upstairs, first the cat but then my son moving around. I don't even have tea, I could offer you some water with mint leaves. Is that your son up there? Why isn't he at…? And then the spiel about him being ill, a nasty cold, the blankets pulled up to his chin. How would I describe our relationship, have we got used to living in a place like this, how do we cope in winter, do we have any extra help, what's our monthly income, our legal status and she studies the clutter, the dust on the trays, the pile of prescriptions, the cold air circling with no heater in sight. We get rid of her with convulsions and an emergency call.

The car motionless outside the vineyards. His trainer prints on the seatbacks, the hubcaps missing in front. Both doors bashed in, the windscreen wipers snapped. Him nowhere to be seen. He's not here, can't you see he's not here, let's go back, he begs. We're almost out of petrol. Let's just go. What are those guys doing over there, using just enough braincells to tie the branches to the wire. How many plants do they tie in one day, winding them round the metal poles, how much do they earn in an hour as they go up and down the rows. I see a few men standing by the stakes. He's not with them. There's a tall guy giving orders from a tower and no one's allowed to speak. Wait, somebody's coming. Is that him in the suit, Mum? No, but he won't be long, he's always the last to leave, a workaholic in the family firm, his father would thrash him if not. The boss directing the workers like a hierarch. They're doing it all wrong, and he calls them over and lays into the old-timers, forty seasons under your belts and now look at you, hands full of useless junk, don't stare at the ground while I'm talking, you slackers, what were your names again, speak up, you can't even tie your shoelaces properly.

It's dark now. My son is snoring unfed. I didn't even buy him some cheesy crisps from the service station machine, or stop at the lookout point so he could take a leak. Maybe I'm making him backward. Maybe there's severe or moderate damage, ma'am they said, ma'am, are you listening, you dropped him a long way, from the changing table, not the high chair but it's all the same, at this age the fontanelle hasn't closed. I promise if he's not out in the next few minutes, we'll go home and I'll make the dinner. But there's a light still on, I know he's in there, I can see him. The workers have left, mumbling apologies, the vineyards at this hour are green arcades. How to find the words. The dew is falling. Where to look for them even. There is nothing more narcotic than this sky.

But the light went out above the vines and he got in his car and sped away, grazing me on the curve. This can't be the end of it. I run to my son, stuff him in the back with twisted legs, claw at the wheel and put my foot down. I'm on his tail but he goes even faster, so do I and I'm right behind him, hand crushing the horn. Then he brakes and I ram straight into him, leaving his bumper and bodywork wrecked. He gets out. Nothing in sight besides two shut shops and the ashes of centuries-old houses. Rocks, peeling roundabouts, a sign for the next town along. And that icy air and that sticky sigh in two bodies that want each other. What the hell is wrong with you. Nothing. Nothing, for God's sake. If it's nothing then why did you stop writing.

And he grabs me. I want to think, to curse, to make accusations. You're kidding me, you're fucking with me. You're doing this on purpose. I try to push him away and talk to him but he's sucking up my oxygen and turning me inside out. He leads me to his air-conditioned car like I'm a cripple. At no point did I remember leaving the headlights on and the engine running. At no point did I remember him asleep in the back with the handbrake off. And just after or before undressing, who knows how but we suddenly lurched, minds gone and then the cars were rolling backwards down the hill, two skating birds seen from above. And it was him who leapt out, tripping over his trousers and lunging for the handbrake. It was him who saved my son. Still red from his beard I drive laden with life, ashamed but so drunk I shriek and kick the accelerator as the boy looks on, slumped in his shuddering seat. Eyes like eggs. I'm in second when the car makes a noise like letting go and starts veering from side to side, as if it's dragging something, tugging something left and right, teetering on a tightrope. Some twenty-ton rabbits go thudding to safety. Back at home I give him something to eat and drink, the plate bubbling on the tray. I go out for firewood, fan the coals hard and throw kindling on the sparks. And then this desire to piss standing up, to vault over the backs of the cattle.

During the day, him at school and me preparing the basket, the entrails, the handful of bullets. I go and pick him up, wait desperate at the gates and when they all come out I practically climb him. More laughter from his classmates but he takes no notice and throws himself into my arms. Let's go hunting, let's feel the bones in our fingers. On the roadside we see cats abandoned by holidaying families, sun loungers strapped to the roof racks and the pets thrown out the windows. And then we're trying on our dungarees, hopping to shake off the cold, tall leather boots so we don't get bitten and old gloves for grip when we shoot or stab. Trousers with pockets, body warmers. Each of us carrying our engraved knife, cord for tying and laying traps, a carabiner to secure the rope in case there's a scramble and a rifle to fire at our prey. Ready for the chase. We roam the scrapyards among cars and stolen motorbikes, heaps of damaged vehicles to be stripped and sold for parts. We skid down a slope in a shower of pebbles, wade in the muddy water and shoot animals out of the sky. It's not hunting season and these aren't hunting grounds, so we try to be discreet. Then finding what falls, front row seats for the death throes. Celebrating each collapse before dragging, hanging, rinsing. The swollen sense of power. We're sitting high up, my son hands back the deep red meat and we wring it out over the stream. Then we drink, him in sugary sips. We drink so much we get hiccups and go rolling down through the valley, over the branches, the red scorpions and plastic bags left by outsiders who come here to fuck.

Alone in the end and waiting, not knowing how to wait by now in this shantytown among half-built rooms, settlers and their clans looking down from the rafters and women busy rearing the rest. The lemony smell of newborn goat, of spiced seeds and herbs. Waiting for him on the tiles in a dress and my leather biker boots. Below the waist one thing but above it a wreck if you listen to my son when he gets pissed off, but slender legs, but pretty shoulder-length hair, but an edible mouth. He'd better be here soon. Closing my eyes, not old enough yet to crash and burn, too young to be a mole living under the pipes or spend my days picking parasites off leaves. A woman comes out with a bowl of breadcrumbs and raises her hand. There he is with the usual signal, make for the narrow lane, climb in quick, no lingering by the main road, no pouncing, no biting. And nothing to talk about afterwards, nothing to say with prickling skin from the cheap fabric and milk-yard vegetables, not a word that fits after touching each other on those luminous bike rides and walks. No one at the school gate. The tall railings padlocked, the cenotaph covered in doodles. Along the tarmac, in the disabled parking where they catcall the social cases, outside the staff entrance, nothing. The slope leading to the hospital, the back of the building, the immigrants' tower blocks. The square with the little outdoor gym and black nannies phoning home to their countries, the concrete walkways where those same phones are resold. The ditch by the roundabout, the skate ramps, the entrance to the sports centre, the area of the riding club for seniors and life members. The indoor pool, the saunas, the private room for swingers and the convicts' gym, the esplanade, the post office, the bar. Nothing. I'm not even that late I say, swearing as I run a red light and the speed bumps shatter the engine. How late could I be when we were checking the time, my mouth full of hair, my mouth full of face, full of his snot, why's he torturing me. The train station on strike, the tobacconist's. Nothing. The retirement district where an old guy took his Kawasaki for one last ride before selling it and ran over a girl just learning to walk. Still nothing. The megastores for the poor full of extra-large jars and unmarked bottles of oil, their coupons held out for a few measly cents off. Not a trace. I can't have been that late to pick him up if when we checked the time we were already sober, feet in our shoes on the boat. I drive home down the motorway, cursing at the empty vault of the sky. Bursts of maternal sobbing. Bursts of uncontrollable shaking. Nests high up like clumpy beehives spoil the view of the grove. I can't have completely forgotten to collect him from the final exam if when he went at me again face to the ground, I said with his saliva in my mouth: I have to go. I have to go. I must have said it ten times. Driving along, eyes straining for a young man who hates his mother. A young man trudging past the vineyards with a skull rucksack and frayed trousers, a young man weaving from left to right and spitting on the ground. The plants offer up their shoots, their sativa smell. I switch on the full beams in case I catch sight of his thighs making the concrete shake. I'm an attacker, son, I always need something to attack. And I know it'll stay with you forever, the day I forgot to pick you up. A murderess in the son's retelling. Deficient in everything. Hands begging for mercy. He's nowhere in sight. Another mother would be checking the morgues among unidentified bodies, the gullies or the bottom of a septic tank. He could be stuck in the scrubland, at a faulty railway crossing, half-trampled by a racehorse or lurking at a checkpoint behind the tyres of the trucks from the North.

I drive slowly, sometimes speeding up and then braking, looking for him like for a lost beaver digging in its incisors. My lightning-bolt son, my comet son. And suddenly in the distance between the dark and the dark there's a hunched-up crow walking along. I get as close as I can so he can't fly away. But he carries on, no stopping until madness sets in. I tumble out running, try to fold him in my arms but he pushes me aside. I stand in his path with a stricken shriek of son but he shoves me again and strides out in front. The house isn't far, the car blocking the road, I stand in his way again, lie down in front of him. He steps straight over me but I'll jump, you just watch me I'll jump, I'll jump and you'll be sorry, all bluff and swagger like a baby soldier with a bomb and he makes a crude gesture. But he doesn't stop or turn to look and if a cattle truck comes round the bend it'll hit us and send him spinning off the road. I stand on two feet, clamber up his bony back but he flicks me off like a weevil and now I'm watching him walk away, hearing him say: I was born from your arse and I've stunk ever since.

I can see something sunken in his eyes. Kneeling on the pavement I try and persuade him to forgive me but I'm bad at making arguments, bad at remembering his childhood. I think he just got a thrill from seeing me ruined at that hour with my bare legs and my forgive me bouncing off the stagnant canals, because he burst out laughing and stopped to examine me. He took me by the hand but first we looked at each other, how can anyone bring forth a look like that. Right, I'm taking you to karate. You have to do something, I have to take you somewhere. When we step into the room with the tatami floor, I see the line of boys in kimonos ready in the basic yellow-belt stance. Padded walls all around and boards hanging level with their heads. There are no other adults in the room so I sit down and become a creature in my lair. My son joins the line. My son the sturdiest, the broadest, the strapping young man takes a Japanese bow. Just like earlier I see him widen his stance, throwing punches and low kicks with panache. I look only at him, now he's kicking high and low, gaze switching between a fixed point and me. Now he's using his fingers, up in the air, nukite, shuto, tsuki, uke, geri, enpi, hiza geri, what the hell is she saying. The instructor teaching him to concentrate and when she follows his eyes she finds me. I like this teenage-boy smell on the mats with the white walls behind, this bare-handed battleground. I look at each one in turn and think which girl they'll go wild for, which girl's throat they'll slit, see the women parading past barefoot. But the powers that be throw me out and I have to go behind the curtain, my hands covered in chalk. A mother spying on what's hers. From back there I recognise his footsteps by their force, read the notices, it's nearly the end-of-year belt presentation. I note down the date but all I care about is him, his muscles, his strength, his feet kicking the air.

On the way out, surprise, where are you taking me he says topless with his white trousers slung low, his bones protruding, surprise I say and cover his eyes until we're at the shop selling mopeds. He walks around looking at prices, gets on one, gets on another, puts his foot on the accelerator, grimaces like a champion racer, studies the grooves in the rubber. I'd better be forgiven after this, you'll be able to come and go as you please. Who's the scooter for, ma'am. For the family I say and the salesman stares like that's not a real word. For you, for your husband, how old's the boy. For everyone, I say. What's the mileage, any crashes, are you guys the owners, are the papers in order, purchase invoice, maintenance logbook, keys, check-ups, road tax, my baby talking like a grown man. Meanwhile I counted the notes in my purse and held up five fingers to show how much we had. And not a cent more, we're eating into our savings I mouth and he smiles back, cool, all good and I get a thumbs up, we'll eat clods of earth for lunch, green corn on the cob, and we leave with the scooter and two helmets. The savings from when your mother was a woman. I follow behind, yelling through the car window for him to stop being an idiot, the old granny bug-eyed by the roadside, watch where you're going or you'll crash. But he keeps swinging his legs, twisting round to pull faces, standing up in the seat. I try to drive alongside but the road's narrow and coiled and at times I'm stuck a few yards behind. Sit down and go slowly I shout, hanging out of the window but he doesn't listen. A team of pro cyclists overtake in single file with numbers on their chests, neon trainers and concave helmets. He cuts them up, the line unravels and they call my son a retard. I try to make him stop but he hurtles ahead, then loses balance and dips to one side. Standing at a junction next to a camera, two police officers signal for him to stop but he barely slows. They blow their whistle, order him to pull over. A few miles later they manage to catch him before he veers off into the vineyards.

I sit waiting for him at the police station, my dress still dirty from the last time. Trying to go unnoticed, hair over my face, but the interrogation still comes. Are you the mother of the boy in for questioning, are you here with him, hanging the sign around my neck and marching me through the streets. Posters on the walls about taking drugs when you're pregnant and pictures of babies deformed in the womb, about alerting the authorities to the sound of gunfire or children held hostage in their homes. Official figures for first-degree burns in the under-tens versus other domestic accidents, drawings of children jumping off cliffs, slitting their wrists or setting the house on fire. You have to check your windows are completely shut, and any doors leading to stairs, says a woman in a headscarf to a younger girl beside her who's invisible except for her eyes. You can't dress like that here, I say, she'll have to take it off before going in, she looks more like a bin bag than a woman. She wants to wear it, the woman replies, she won't go to school bare-headed, what am I supposed to do. People can wear what they like, ma'am, another woman says, that's how democracy works. And they all stare at my laddered tights and the muddy heels of my shoes. When a police officer calls me I get up, stumble and enter the room, where they run through the latest infractions. We avoid each other's eyes on our plastic chairs. The mother and son's criminal record updated, with details of the incidents and the endless warnings from social services. They shake our hands, dispensing advice, and show us to the door. Eat, lad, they seem to say, you look malnourished. My son stares at the outlined eyes of the girl shrouded in black.

Him at the wheel, me leaning back all trussed up in my seatbelt, cutting off my blood flow, there'll be a fine for the scooter that no one will pay. The car carries on down the road. I watch the sheep at high speed as they glitter on the ice, haunches wrapped in ravelled wool that turns to tulle, turns to pearls. I never want to go home. Don't stop, I tell him, drive, just drive, the flashing lights announcing changes of region, accidents, terrorist threats, keep driving, straight through the barriers. We go faster and faster, the sheep's bodies white sharks gliding in and out of the water.

The village covered in snow, the cat at the window showing signs of frostbite but I still don't let it in. I watch through the glass for some hint of distress but the cat just slides its eyes to meet mine. If it moves it can come in, if it scratches the pane, if it meows, if it's able to stand. It can come in even if it just twitches its tail. But it does nothing, allowing its muscles to seize up and the wind to freeze its flesh. Then I turn away, put it out of my mind, begin trailing after my son like a drunk. One step forwards and one step back. Slurring a word now and then but the boy understands, you understand me right I say, yes, yes, I understand everything. I order him about, come on, give your teeth a good brush, ten times up and ten times down, plus your gums so you won't need braces, now go and tidy the dinosaurs in your room and he looks at me with pity in his eyes. I follow his footsteps around the house, forwards, back, up the stairs placing my prints in his, down again after him, and when he goes into the bathroom he slams the door in my face. I wait for him, shadow him out to get firewood and into the kitchen where he boils some pasta. I'm his cloud, his perdition. I see myself against the creepers that cling to the bricks of long-demolished houses. Like in the cheap canteens and silos, the stench animals leave. Like poultry scratchings, like the murk of the cattle in the slaughterhouse truck. And with my son's back still turned in the steam from the stove I can suddenly see myself dying.

Starlight. I have no idea what the thing is and for a moment I stare at it blankly. Perplexed by that ball formed in front of me. That doll like a gift from a man in love. That layered shape fattened by the overnight snow. My son gets out of bed in his boxers and yells. We pull on the old boots from back when I took him skiing on the mountain, the woolly socks full of holes, the fluorescent thermal jackets. We take it in turns to bash it with an axe but the body is slow to appear. I toss him the frosty scarecrow and he sends it back, I throw it in his face this time and he lobs it at my chest. We play catch for a while, hands in gloves until the cat comes loose, but we can't bring ourselves to bury it deep underground or send it into the void.

There's a commotion. No one ever looks out, not since they rationed the lighting and it cuts off at midnight like a whip on a horse. No one stirs any more, not even a quick trip out for rolling tobacco. Impossible to move from one field to another, past cars diagonal-parked on private vegetable plots. But my son sticks his head through the first-floor window. Some girl in black, he says, and lights her up with the laser I won at the fête. And first all I see is our kisses on winning and I can't hear a thing, the kisses smother the room, there's a woman in black coming this way and crying. You don't get black people here, I say, don't be ridiculous. We've never seen her before, she's not one of our neighbours but she's striding past the houses, she knows where she's going, never hesitating or losing her way. I can't see much but I think she's covering her face. We light her up and she's ducking and weaving, a woman destroyed. We light her up better and she looks at our window. Shit. We duck. We're laughing hysterically but I get the pepper spray just in case, shame I didn't buy the value pack with the cattle prod. She's seen us, he leans out but I yank him back. We hear her knocking at the house opposite, but then right away she's crossing to where we are. Turn that off, and I snatch back the laser. We're both giggling from the rush of seeing someone else suffer, someone else despair and beg for help before our very eyes. Our nipples hard, our necks tense. She has a weird way of speaking but makes herself understood. My son gets up and goes downstairs, and for a second I stay behind swathed in kisses. Kisses, kisses, hell itself. Kisses, kisses more kisses, a warren of kisses. The teenager in underpants reaches the ground floor.

She's got herself beaten up. What do I do. And I hear them talking through the door, her pleading for political asylum. This isn't some kind of holding centre. Another window lights up. And another. And another over there. Tattletales. Someone coming for her. I hate this woman who's dragged me downstairs before breakfast. Should I let her in? Where would we put her? Pandemonium outside like a riot in a dog pound. A riot of neighbours calling the police. I take the cap off the pepper spray. What the hell is wrong with you. We should let her in, she's shivering, there's something coming out of her chest. She tries to squeeze through the bars but she doesn't fit. He turns the key. The woman outside pressed up against the door, I can practically feel her secretions. They'll come and burn the place down with us inside, I say, the louts will cover it in swastikas. This isn't the city, this isn't some jungle gym for illegal immigrants and I turn the key the other way. She begs me woman to woman, what do I care if she's a woman. You can go round the back, the bushes are tall, get down on the ground and don't move. My son takes the key and puts it in the lock but I snatch it back and stuff it in my jailer's pocket. The woman hurries towards the garden and is almost round the corner when a hand grabs her by the throat.

No trace of the episode after breakfast and we don't mention the woman again. Just once I think I see her flat out in the hedge mustard, but no one says anything and that's the end of that, like the unmarked graves or the school bus that nosedived into the river. We're painting the window frames green when I see him get out of his car and for the first time the three of us are together. But it's fine, it's natural and I show him off to my son like a garland. Right away he helps us finish. Look what I've got myself. I've been useless all along but look. Look at this man, I want to tell him so he sees. I go to the market and make straight for the insecticides, leaving the two of them to finish the sanding, add a second coat and put back the frames. On my way out I hold tight to the sight of them squatting among the anemones. I bet the old hags in the chapel feel horny like this when they're checking out the relics.

I come back and the windows are drying propped among the chairs. I can smell the two of them through the fresh paint, showered and attacking the anthill by the pool. Mum, he's got a technique for getting rid of the ants, it's no use massacring them, you have to leave them half-dead so they give off a chemical that frightens the others and warns them of the danger. Look, he says, pointing as they writhe around and the others scuttle away. I leave them to it, fix a snack, bottles of mint drink for the boy, beers and aguardiente for us. Making them something to eat, watching my hands as they do it. The three of us laughing around the white cast-iron table. Now and then him stroking my forearm or shoulder mid-sentence, laying his hand on me when my son can't do the same, now and then the air between them severed. And me expansive, joyous, not shut away or tooth and nail in a catfight. The bottles empty, we go for a stroll through his vineyards past blackcurrants and cherries and he tells him all about managing the winery, production, storage, quality control before moving on to bottling and sales. I drift behind them narcotic on the scent of leather, moss, game, and beyond that incense, camphor, resin, pine, toast, smoked coffee. We walk straight into a wine-tasting festival, wander the clammy stone passageways with tasting notes on the walls. Now and then he drags me down to the cellar, we glug and glug while his staff paw at him, thanking him. Merci, merci, sir, through the underground alleys. Each of us roaming the tunnels alone, downing the dregs as we go. It's morning by the time we emerge, drunk, and blow into the breathalysers, failing miserably but everyone smiles at the boss. My son's nodding off, but in the truck he perks up and we put on some music, anything in English will do, and we're just another local family of winos.

A blissful kiss outside the farmyard as he sleeps squashed into the back. Hundreds of ducks are running around bellowing and he tells me how people stick tubes down their throats and force them to eat, breaking their necks to turn their livers to fat. How they're tortured, stuffed full of slop till they choke, and all because they can't vomit. Then in we go and the farmer lets us sample two kinds of foie gras on freshly-baked homemade bread. The taste smeared on our tongues, we kiss again and again. In the car with the windows iced over, he lowers his trousers. Is he still breathing back there, how can you tell. Then he's pushing me and I'm pushing harder like I'm pushing at a solid mass, my whole body against a toppling truck. I push to send him flying, enmeshed like ivory antlers I'm pumping in the face of death. We follow the road to where it skirts the cliff. I want him to speed up and send us somersaulting into the fields or down to the islands, the boats tied together, the surfacing dunes. I start shaking, not yet a seizure, gaze still steady but then a twitch in my colourless eyes. A police car drives past. Who knows what I've done but an officer gets out and asks if I need any help. I can't control my tongue. I start pedalling from side to side on the ground and end up spreadeagled face-down. They take me to the emergency room. I'm in no fit state to drive. When they ask who's responsible for the boy, he says he is. Through the glass I see low 1970s buildings, retirement homes with red eaves, amusement parks, the pensioners' bowling green, period costumes in the shops, and men leaning out of their guillotine windows, using as little as they can of their lives.

You have to sit down by the dead in the room with the sharpened sound and the knocking on the glass. I listen to the monitor system and try to harmonise with the refrain. But I'm too desecrated, I've fallen too far. I don't know what to do, I fight, persist, the nurses give me higher doses, medical novelties to no avail. I can't speak properly. The treatments don't work, people always say it takes time. A new switch in my life, a socket in the middle of my chest. At the mercy of an artery, a spasm, a bone. What's the matter with me, I ask them both, in their chairs facing the bed. What is it. But they say nothing, they exchange glances. In the room: scanner, radio and the blood test tonight. Two unexplained seizures so far today and the gallons of medicine hit like a bullet. Most people in their final moments are like a monkey waving from a palm tree. This is the truth behind the rumours, we all have plans, we all want to go higher, we're all counting on our fingers what little sex we have left. And higher still. All of us all of us. Higher and higher. I call the doctors who come running, roll up their sleeves and then melt away. Monkeys unmoored. It's too dark here and it's horrible, this is how you break a man, a piece at a time.

40.8 on the thermometer. I don't know what to do. I call the doctor on duty but what's the point if he'll only look gormless like the one in the emergency room and the neurologist, no point trying another specialist or department. In this hospital they wheel you off for a morning X-ray and your brain thinks movement therefore transfer, stimulated by the changes from one floor to the next. The face of a nurse starting her shift, the fumes from the food or the staff scurrying past with sweat-soaked sheets. Now they're taking me back down to my floor in the lift, I see someone worse off and I don't pretend, a few more hours and another immigrant will be tucked up in that bed. The new arrivals don't pretend with me either, they stare and

I can see it in their eyes. So long, grandma, you washed-up old hag, time to make room for us in this country.

Again the same long day of not lifting a finger, aside from ensuring I breathe I don't exert myself at all. I woke up asking my son if he wasn't meant to be at karate. The karate display I yelled and they took me out with a slingshot. Then they went to the kebab stand, the only place around here that seems to think the healthy need feeding as well. Two hours later, both chairs empty, they'll be drinking aperitifs in a betting shop or touring the casinos. I fall asleep to the beeping. Watch the door in case it opens. Still no idea what's happening, a resident now in this wretched place. The other patients on my floor leave their slippers in the doorways like beasts of burden.

I'm going to punch the next clinician who walks in, all these young men greedy for weird pathologies, their excitement visible a mile off with every juicy case. Doctor, there are high levels of lead in my body and it's poisoning my brain, which might explain the damage to the frontal lobes, please get rid of all this metal inside me. Quickly if it's not too much trouble, the fits are so frightening. Like internal whiplash. Try this cheese. That was painful, right?

Did you like it? Now this other one, have a taste, no ill will, and then spinal taps, scans, MRIs, X-rays and EEGs. The lights left to flicker in the market below. I feel like one of those wartime chancers who pull out old coins to pay for the train. My strength seeping away like the hours in the trenches with bombs overhead. My heart beginning to race. Why are other people out there in peak condition, savouring liqueurs, why have I landed down here? Why am I not at the bottom of a ravine, in a shanty-town sickroom, an ambulance stuck in traffic on the bypass. I'm roused from what I thought was thought by the sweet sound of delirium. The first time it had me screaming for the hospital director, but now I can manage by myself. Each floor has a different rhythm. A car passes outside, an ambulance pulls away and runs a red light. The Santa from last Christmas hangs on the wall, grinning and winking, causing accidents, amputations, nothing serious.

One day they discharge me having understood nothing and I can eat and speak again. The file signed, stamped. No major neurological problems, ma'am, just damage from various incidents. Am I free to go? I vacate the bed. I vacate the room and someone's pushing their way in behind. Good luck, my undocumented friend, I say and he glares back with chlorinated eyes. He'll have been picked up somewhere in a state of shock, stammering when they ask his name, racking his brains till they make up a new one. I'm out of the building by sunrise. We leave arm in arm. I see the three of us on a frozen expanse, crossing the continent with the help of a cane.

We all make it home, and if it weren't for the smell and our pasty skin, we could almost be returning from Corsica. The minor dazed after the ordeal, several days on the trot and a hospital finish, like a big wedding where the bride and groom wind up at the first-aid centre in their fancy clothes and straw hats. Right, get some sleep and then off to school he says and they were a couple of guys slapping palms, bumping fists. I waited outside till my son was in bed. He should go to school more often, you know. This week he'll go every day, it goes in phases. Last year he had perfect attendance. His education does not go in phases. You should make sure he's on time. I can never get him out of bed and I'm no morning person either. But you should, he says, and in a flash I see his neck scratched raw from an attempted strangulation. Silence. We're two farmyard ducks. If you ask me, this relationship isn't even the most important thing happening around our lives today, or at least not now, or not around mine. Hang on a second, I don't understand, around what? I mean we should be taking care of other urgent things that are slipping away. Like your son, who's clearly directionless, or my business, which falls to bits when I'm not there. I've been neglecting my work lately. It's like that with wine, it must be like that with a kid. And look where we ended up, you in hospital, seizures because of me. I'd better be going. You can tell him to come and work with me next summer, the money's right for a kid his age and there's always room on the payroll. Then he can cover his costs in the holidays and hang out with other boys his age. Plus he should take up a sport, he's always so pale, so weak. Now give your mind a rest, which is what the doctor said, and he kisses me on the forehead.

A mental short-circuit, my whole spirit sliced off. I let him go, I lose contact. Depression takes the reins. I look at him like a barren woman devouring a friend's rosy baby with her eyes. Like watching close-up as a line of chicks get sucked down a pipe to the sewers. Losing him the ultimate nightmare, waking up a new dawn, watching the cold air travel from the door to the window, not having him, staring out as the earth turns over, as someone walks by along the edge of the field, as a kestrel dozes on its feet. Getting up the next day and destroying my heart as it contracts. Then the involuntary movements kick in and carry me along.

By the morning I know what happened but I still can't understand it. I make him breakfast and if the pair of them had switched faces in the night I wouldn't even notice. I take him to school, moving like a machine. He's not talking either, who knows why not. My son still has numbered boxes where he keeps my photos, my albums, my magazine covers, my necklaces and pairs of my stockings. Then a day spent staking out the school. I go into a diner for factory workers from the industrial estate and lorry drivers from the East, but when I sit down with my tray, my food and my fizzy drink, the gag reflex has me staggering outside. I wait for home time, clumsily crossing each road on a roundabout while the drivers drum their fingers, or walking among houses built on stilts so the water doesn't wash them away. I wait for him to come out, wandering past shisha bars, apple, vanilla, never thinking once about what happened. I pause by a small group slouched on some benches. Gypsies will make this country explode one day if they keep blocking pipes, setting cables alight and letting their kids loose in the road. Pumped full of wine, cesspits for mouths. I sit down nearby and the winter sun is like a mental state. They make me drink. I watch the Gypsies race up and down the tunnel used by delivery lorries. Every so often they throw a stone and out drops a package or a couple of cans. The place is full of Eritreans, Poles, reoffending Syrians. We're fucked for all eternity. They don't ask what I'm doing or how I ended up there. It's full of Jews, we never saw them but they came. A vehicle with foreign plates pulls out of the car park. Go back to your own countries, all of you, they shout, I try to sidle away but one of them grabs me and clasps me to his chest. They give me a gun and I imagine aiming at him and emptying the barrel but then they take it back. The car comes closer, circles the roundabout, indicates right and drives straight past. I could swear it's him but I persuade myself it's not, and when a fight breaks out I make my escape. They go en masse to raid the supermarket dumpsters, to gorge themselves on gone-off food, to face the police and security guards who chase them away with tear gas while they retaliate with boleadoras. Final stop, the bins to steal out-of-date medicines before they're shipped off to Africa or burnt on a pyre while the authorities turn a blind eye. One of them spots me and shouts for me to join them. On the next street along I count the cash in my rucksack to see if anything's missing, that lot would pinch a necklace in a heartbeat. I add up my welfare payments and empty my bank account, do the sums on my fingers, go over my savings and wait.

The teacher wants a word. The principal, too. Fine, I'll come back another day, let's get going. No, Mum, now, they're waiting inside. But I can't go in now, have you lost your mind? Look at my clothes, my hair's a state, I'm not wearing any make-up, come on, we're going, I've got news. But they're waiting in the principal's office, it's urgent. They couldn't get hold of you. It's switched off, I didn't charge it, I don't know where the charger ended up, you know I never remember to charge it. Okay but I said you'd go in for a minute, I could go with you or wait out here. And I don't move. I've never been inside your school before and he gave me a push, come on and we walked down the hallway, the classrooms on either side full of the chaos and light from the last lessons of the day. We turn a corner and there they are, two people who show me in and tell him to wait outside. I sit down with my head in my hands. And they talk about his repeated and unacceptable absences, his strange moods, how he's a loner and comes to school hungry, how he gets teased by his classmates, and some rumours about me. Apparently we've been spotted peeling off price tags in shops. I look at the window, outside winter departing, not one bird on the church domes or castle turrets as my son paces up and down. It's my turn to speak. Having to say something with a swollen brain. With swollen genitals, like a woman or a pet dead set on feeling foetal movements, breasts growing like crazy but with nothing there, nothing, people keep telling them, nothing whatsoever. And you can see it all. A swirl of words and I plunge headlong but God knows what I'm saying. I can't look at them either. They ask me to come back the next day to see a committee of parents, educational supervisors and pedagogical directors. They weren't satisfied with my explanation. Outside I grab his arm and say please can we go. I show him the cash in my rucksack pocket and suggest the bar with the green awning in town. We sit at one of the little tables on the pavement, flower-shaped sesame biscuits and lemon beer, this place used to be busy but now it's just me and all these men. My son feeling awkward. I ask if I'm being inappropriate as I sip my aperitif. The waiter shrugs before stacking the chairs on the tables and kicking us out. There aren't any women on the promenades either, or in the pharmacies or shoe shops and it's not even night. A city of men. That's when I tell him I need help, that he has to come with me. We stop to buy margherita pizza from the family with the truck by the motorway but he still doesn't get it, he wants to go home. Children always want to go home. I take the weight off his back, it's still not dark, we have to wait. Would you live like that with me, he says, and we imagine ourselves holed up in a caravan in the desert. Would you live like that till the end, I ask. And we sit on the bridge with two fizzy drinks and read the spray-painted mobile numbers of girls who'll suck you off, our legs hanging down as the trailers pass by and the steam rises out of the drain. He asks what the teacher and principal said. It's fine, I tell him, people won't talk about me any more, it was all just gossip. But what were they saying. I stare at the machinery, the huge metal wheels, what were they saying about you he asks. And at the hospital, did he say he was planning to leave me? We didn't talk at the hospital. But what did he say? Could you tell he was up to something? Did you see any signs? Honestly, none? You can usually tell. The time comes and they feel the beginnings of a chill in the soles of their feet. Let's get out of here. Where to, the shadow of his long chicken legs follows me down the pavement. Where to.

Parked in front of a big chalet with a sweeping roof, we can see lights on inside, two cars and behind them a jeep. On the steps to the basement, a tower of cardboard boxes, and some soot blowing out of the chimney. Hardly any, the final specks after the embers have dulled. Come on, I say, let's find some stones down there to throw. Zero response. Let's throw stones at the house, the cars, the front door, the yappy little dog if they have one, then we'll get back in and clear off. It won't take more than five minutes, I've worked it all out, but I can't do it by myself. I need your arms. Mum, if you do that I'm leaving and never coming back. I'll run away, I don't care, I'll live wherever, do anything, swing through the jungle or malinger at motorway services. And he climbs in the passenger seat. We stay like that for a while, crickets filling the silence, but I still don't start the engine. Inside the house the lights change places and turn gold. The front door opens and a dog bounds out. Phone him. Phone him and be done with it. That's all you need to do if you can't drive away. Phone and tell him to come out, make up an excuse, a work thing, I can go if that helps and say I'm an employee, whatever, but get on with it because I've got stuff to do for tomorrow. I call, it rings, I wait, my eyes on his polished architect's house. Hi. I'm outside, I need to talk to you, it won't take long. I can't come out, he says, it's not just me here tonight. My son can knock at the door and I'll hide behind the hedge. I can't, okay? Never come here again and he hangs up. I stare at the windscreen wiper stopped halfway, the glass marked on one side, pristine on the other. And I start the engine. He pulls out the key and slowly opens the door. I hear his plastic boots come down one by one on the leaves. Off he goes, stooping, crouching, crawling, disappearing from view. My limbs slack with exhaustion. I see a figure return, T-shirt full, and he drops stones of all sizes next to me. My soldier son. Phone again. I do as he says, he's thinking for me. I phone, no answer. I look at him. Phone again, go on, he commands. Do it. I phone. Switched off. I tell him. Switched off? My son hands me a stone. Together we get out and find a spot near the French windows and skylights. The first one lands like a cruise missile over a hill, then he throws the next, the biggest and it smashes their living-room window. We hear shrieking, swearing. Rapid footsteps, furniture being moved around. And we send in more stones, stones fired from the slingshot, stones aimed at their faces like a shower of fireworks, big stones, small stones and as they're pulling shut the curtains and lowering the blinds, we hit the kitchen window and the whole thing shatters. Inside they're running in circles, dragging more stuff around, yelling for us to stop or they'll call the police. We fire several at a time until our arms cramp up, we're in terrible shape, there's a light coming towards us down the road.

He's awoken by the crash of broken crockery hurled into the forests. Bottles whirling, full and empty, detonating all around. Hands that smell of a heavy night. Now what, he says from his bed. Now what. The woman who gave birth to me and never lets me rest. The woman who made me has lost it completely and come to corner me still horny from her night. Too early to walk without squinting or carrying a torch. Early enough to mistake an Alsatian for a fierce mud-encrusted bear, or the first glint of sun behind the trees for a wildfire. I pretend I'm doing things, watch myself doing them, tidy cups, haul wardrobes open and shut. I'm about to leave when my son stands in my way and says let's get out of here. Let's clear off for a bit till the offensive stops. Maybe he's told the police, or his contacts. Law enforcement breathing down our necks. But if we're going we need to go right now, before one of his lackeys shows up.

We should camp out in one of his childhood summers, sit off to one side nibbling cold potato salad and crab while other children run downhill carrying nuts. I don't know how to say sorry. We should play cards on the tablecloth behind the caravan. And next winter the chimney would be cleaned in time and there'd always be firewood to fritter away and prunes in the copper pan for homemade jelly. And cowboy costumes and toy guns tied at the waist and armour around the children's chests. But instead this uncontainable fury across furrowed fields, groves of trees and every few miles a tantrum, wanting to turn back and him always pushing us on. We take the straightest road. Why are we doing this? Feeling we've put at least a few villages behind us, but then sometimes a suspicion we're just circling the house, the animals staring, telling us we've got nowhere. The trees are all the same, they blur in the wind and the landscape is erased. We don't pass anyone else. On either side we see grimy waterlogged handbags, tin cans, dresses and summer hats floating down the stream. Sacrifices, discarded lives. We don't know if we're making progress or when night's going to fall. I ask if he's hungry and give him the one thing

I brought, bread and tuna, momentarily smug for remembering lunch, for feeding him like when they said I was expecting a boy, so much better begetting the opposite sex, producing a man, a person who will one day be stronger, more capable, who will carry you in his arms down rocky paths or shield you with his flesh. Under the slabs the rodents growl. We sit down for a rest in a lean-to on what looks like a Nordic farm resort. We haven't seen it before but that doesn't mean we've come any further than our neighbour's backyard. I stretch out, say good night without thinking and he doesn't respond, just lets me rest my head on his forearm like a rifle.

Now I have him on top of me. I look at the tall, unmoving trees, how do they produce their inanimate life. Fear of being seen. Fear of wanting him to stay there. Eventually I push him off and he's lying face-down, one hand squashed beneath his stomach, his mammal mouth desperate to drink. Was he shot by hunters or did he climb on of his own free will. I step out from under the roof and there's nothing but mooing in the air. My plan to set off alone but he gets up and follows. Where are you going, Mum? For a walk. And he sticks to me, stepping on my heels all the way down the path. His fingers brushing against me as we run. Something he always used to do but now doesn't seem right. I stop. You didn't say we should leave just to keep me away from him? I start jogging again. What is wrong with you, he shouts. You were throwing bottles at the cows, you'd have got us evicted, you'd have torn the whole house down. And what about you, dropping out of school and the social worker saying it's my fault. The teachers' fingers stabbing at my temples. I'll go back to school, Mum. Yes, and the police will come along accusing me of neglect, they'll parade me through the vineyards with a sign around my neck, bad mother coming through. But it's you who won't study, you who wants to be illiterate, who'd rather be begging outside bus stations or roadside motels. He catches me up and clings, wants to walk shoulder to shoulder. You'll end up flogging handbags. Propositioning old men. I'll get you out of here, he says in a harmless voice. Let's not talk about my future now, let's concentrate on yours. The lethal voice of the boy who loves. So on we go through pastures of pesticides and hormones but three steps later I can't resist another shot. Maybe you want me to forget him. If he's not in my sightline, if I can't reach out and touch him. And now, how many miles do you think we've come? These luminous times we live in. Let's go back. Not today. No one goes back in the dark. I'm going back I said, but immediately wished I hadn't and hugged him as we walked. I wouldn't leave you. He stopped, prolonging the hug. You're so beautiful, Mum. I want to go back, I'm sorry, forever asking his forgiveness, I'm the worst traveller ever. First we need to sleep, find somewhere to eat, have a wash. A wash? Now? We don't even like switching on the boiler in winter and you're talking to me about washing? But where are we I begin to despair, looking at clouds, flying rats, on the hunt for a landmark. Where are we my son yells and starts running, and I let him go. I'm driving him mad, I'm sorry, but why did he bring me all the way here, what gave him the idea of taking me there, and why as he sprints around trying to get his bearings do I feel as if I'm putting on a show. I act like it's all under control. Like I haven't said anything. He comes back slick with perspiration. I don't know where we are, I can't see any path in or out, tripping over the words. Which way do you think we should go. You didn't recognise anything, I shouted, nothing at all, nothing, not the tiniest thing, a walkway, a wasteland, a shack. And I'm shouting at him, shouting rigid with rage and shaking him because how dare he say nothing, how dare he not give me a foothold. Right, the first car I see, the first person, we'll ask which way to walk over the fields of corn and daffodils. Only one thing matters, and that's getting home before the sun goes back down. We can't be far, we're probably just round the corner, but there's nothing familiar, no tow trucks, no labourers. Not the slightest apparition, no cyclists, no camper vans, no one's being raped down by the pond, the north wind between their legs. No electric hum of a generator, nothing beyond this green seclusion. We decide it must be midday, earth in our hair. I start running, can't bear putting one foot in front of another, counting the petals as I go. For no more reason than hate. And not long after he's running as well and that makes two of us hating it all. At last we spot some gangly kids milling around a pond and on the fringes a herd of cows. Easy targets so we can work out where we are, we're right by the school, the part behind the playground and the classrooms just over the fence. The school, the school we yell and jump up and down. The fucking school, we charge at each other and he gives me a peck like when he was little, I close my eyes and return it runny-nosed. From here they look exactly like a band of sickly urchins. And then we're galloping along, gathering such momentum.

we glide. Virulent joy, a kid on the church roof mooning the faithful. Virulent happiness, an air rifle firing at a flock of birds squashed flat against the glass.

I don't feel bad, should I feel bad? I don't feel the slightest bit bad about making him go to school looking like a tramp. And I set off on foot, sticking my thumb out now and then as if I'd ever be picked up in this state. So another hour trudging uphill, filling the time with fantasies of being freshly washed and hanging out to dry. On the approach, I hear more barking than usual. And no calls of greeting when I reach my farm, which seems odd. No open doors or windows. And outside the house the smell of something rancid fermenting. The whole place turned upside-down and trampled underfoot, a pack of wild cats on the stairs. Grab some bags, throw it all away, find the phone and call him. Track him down whether or not he's the one who let the zoo in. Upstairs my son's room untouched, but mine is upended. I do what I can, back and forth with the bin bags and air freshener to make the place feel like a home. Maggots heaped up on all sides.

I have a wonderful mother, I know I do, you're so wonderful Mum, I was thinking it all the way home. What a wonderful mum, thinking of you all my life, thinking of Mum and giving her presents, an eager child cutting up craft paper. I've been kicked out of school and now I'm free, I have to start from scratch in the year below. I didn't learn anything, I didn't read anything, I never made friends, half the class have no idea who I am. I didn't even get a nickname but whatever, who cares, I'll work something out in the future, and we sit down and dinner's off and for a long time we don't eat a thing. How about living somewhere else next year, a cabin in the south, I'll build it myself, hand-selecting every beam. Or another continent, settle on an island on planks of wood. We live in this enchanted house but late at night, Mum, when I'm alone in bed and I hear you rinsing the tips of your hair, painting your skin or trying to sleep, all these notions take hold of me, like why am I your son? Right that's enough, I cut him off. How long will this last? How long will this feeling go on? My nervous system brimming but I put on a brave face. How do you feel about me, son? Do you feel the way I feel? We could be feeling the same thing right now. I ask myself that endlessly and never get an answer. And you're the one who's losing, what have you done, you gave birth to me and here I am, I understand you, I can help you find your way back. I know where your head was at when you had me, I was hardly out and you were thinking of the soldiers playing football with newborns, tossing them up in the air. I'm just thankful you never sent me away. I listen, patient, as he talks and talks but out there on this frosty night the sordid race is still being run.

He'll want the girls who haven't been born yet, kiss them shyly at first and then with tongues right here in the living room and I'll have to watch, sitting in this chair, serving them refreshments or turning out the light. And another day he'll put one in the back and drive along this same horizon, past the villages and wine cellars, doing it all without any rush, without any retching angst. But now he's kissing me and we're coming undone, not mother and son but two illegals who cross paths in the back of beyond, shellshocked on the roof of some compound. Two punks crossing Europe and foraging in dumpsters, France, Germany, Italy, bins overflowing with half-eaten sandwiches, pastries and unopened biscuits. And as we move further north, Poland, nothing, not even a crust of stale bread. It had to happen, anything can happen in the love between mother and son, why not wait till one day it's all over and then a memory like a non-memory in this calloused house, a hidden miniature replica, a mistaken minute in the snow, a muddle of generations, who's making small talk in the kitchen and who's six feet underground. Someone leads me by the shoulders, the drift ongoing, sugar bowls and pills. The sound of engines shakes us from the state of this monster house, he drags himself off the mattress and leaves. Grabs his rucksack, clothes inside out, labels dangling, a ruffian, gets on the moped and weaves his way through the cattle. Shouting in English *fuck the world, war is business, kill releases* like some kid who hates everything, despises everything, his birth, his age, his raw-boned body, his mother and his lengthening face. The others set off at full tilt.

They ride away, their exhaust pipes waking the families, with him their new conscript. I stand up and walk through the house, still not dressed. I'm no more than the sound of an insect's wing. Old age is a shipwreck.

A yard for stockpiling the ends of lives like clapped-out racing cars. To be able to hang from the smallest, feeblest tree, its roots loose in the soil, and float there all summer, feet over the bamboo pool. To sleep for days and wake swamp-mouthed, take shortcuts through stinging nettles, bare legs bright. To be able to scale something, slide down a spiderweb, electrocute doorknobs with the touch of your hand. My son won't pick up my scent any more, the last river wind will have blown it away. My motherless son, how fast is he going along the ravines, what will those sick junkies do to him. What will they be showing him, a green-painted bison trapped on a school bus till he loses his mind, and a finger up the arse. They'll have him smashing the locks on the bourgeois chalets, raiding the fridges in the budget bungalows, splashing the pensioners, emptying their pockets, forcing the veterans to reel off their exploits. And who knows what else, those delinquents with their hipflasks of vodka, their curdled sleep in the forests of fine white pines that border the campsites. Sneaking in among the tents in the dead of night, rummaging through everything, overturning gas canisters and shouting police, police, kidnapping Dutch girls they find playing in the doorways of rented rooms. They'll teach him it's fun to borrow children and let rip in the backs of the trailers.

I duck underwater to smooth out the creases in my scalp. I'm that test-tube baby. The unstable mother who fought year after year for illegal in vitro abroad is bathing her newborn and it slips from her hands. Then the call to emergency services, they rush the body to the resuscitation room and it's intubated for days before everything ends. She informs her family of her careless behaviour and then scatters it in the Himalayas. And travelling back on her low-cost flight she feels as if the baby never existed. It has no name, no birth certificate, no one even saw it, it's never spoken of again. I come up for air. The sound of a helicopter. I put on scent, adornments, make-up, stretch, go upstairs and start sorting my son's boxes of my stuff, aiming for chronological order. Dresses, perfumes, glory. It's not yet dawn and the army's pea-green contraption is still circling above, training its beam on our rooftops. I go into the garden, stomach empty, and watch. Some people are peering out of their kitchens, hands in the air. Others run down the street, burning with bullets from enemy lines. The light still sweeping the travellers' field, a laser on the crops and the farming machines. People swimming to safety, overcrowded tents, litter everywhere, no one's brave enough to go in. I pick some shiny redcurrants. Tomorrow the wires will be cut, the wells filled in and they'll be marched off the land, the children kept separate but they'll be back, digging up the wells and swinging from the cables. I pick all the gleaming currants, my nails stained red. Back to lobbing their empties at the motorway. Land offensive, aerial attack, reconnaissance, container lorries or a rifle with infrared light, people love a bit of action. I loiter outside and look at the houses. They're all locked up for the dog days, shutters fastened, wooden blinds cracked, metal bolts rusting, mould in the flowerbeds and sickly flowers creeping through the gaps. I hear whispering, the delinquents return, two in clown masks wielding axes or long-bladed knives. My son does his job as the new recruit, keeping watch for kids on scooters or pensioners strolling with folded arms, old men in jackets and flannel shirts, retired lycée teachers who still like to pace with their hands clasped behind their backs. Then the gang spring out and ambush them, waving their knives. The kids flounder, bewildered, but the old men are resigned. I sit in this chair from the morning when the fruit-seller comes until the sun goes all the way down. I never get bored, I don't need to catch radio waves or say things out loud, I simply sit in my chair. I sit and watch the hovering helicopter as if it's just more of the sky.

You're wearing a lot of make-up, says a boy with a stringy beard and baggy clothes. Excuse me, do I know you, I enquire from my sun lounger. No, but you're wearing too much make-up, it's not right. How dare you tell me what's right and what's not, where have you come from, are you new around here. You should only wear make-up for your husband, and I stare at him, scratching myself. He looks at my crotch, my shoulders, then leaves, not without turning his head.

My son comes home the next morning like a dutiful husband, no idea what day of the week it is or what the weather's like outside. Without asking who for, he does up my necklace, buttons my dress, sometimes pressing his lips to my corset. You're stunning. My days as a model in whitewashed village halls, beauty pageants in provincial towns. My days posing for seamstresses, tailors, seasoned photographers, walking and turning, looking into the spotlight. Uninhibited days, bring me the paper and a drink, and the flirting, the flustered gaze of workers, drivers, pilots, in the street, on trains with lascivious ticket inspectors. How do I look, and I pout for him, shameless, walk resplendent to and fro. His eyes restoring my youth, answering my prayers, I'm a slut all over again. I get on the back and we set off to meet him as if we'd made a date. The enormity of seeing him before me. You look perfect, like in that painting only life-size. Like when you couldn't even go to the shops in your dressing gown or house clothes because no one would recognise you and you owed it all to them, and when they stared I was so jealous I could have squashed their eyes like grapes. I laughed. How was your outing, what did they do to you? Nothing, Mum. The providential moment of seeing him again.

The bar owner sells the couple drink after drink. A child sleeps on the counter, head next to the glasses of mint leaves, and the other one, younger, runs around with a spit-soaked handkerchief. People dance in Arabic, people photograph themselves in the frosted mirrors, people climb up and balance on makeshift stages. I wait at the back of the room in a velvet armchair, long-beaked herons on the circular cushions. I wait without touching my crème de cassis, courtesy of the house. I wait breathing my perfume. My son sits across from the baby, drinking a milkshake. Some vineyard workers are celebrating the start of the grape harvest. The sound of them sniffing the wine, holding it on their tongues, swirling their glasses and swallowing it down. The taps open. The bottles on display. Two in the morning and the couple show no sign of leaving or slackening their pace. The child on the counter curls up in a corner. The other huddles between the legs of his bull-faced, beer-bellied alcoholic father. My son finishes his milkshake. I hear the delinquents outside, hissing and whistling. And off he goes, not even glancing back to check it's okay. I sit in my armchair, a human vase. The restaurant looks like a ski lodge with its hairpin beams, stuffed roebuck head and rhinoceros-leg table. All the owners are here except him. Someone passes my son a pipe to smoke. Outside they celebrate his presence, dance around him in circles, tattoo him with fire and make him one of them. Inside, the two brothers, their parents at the bar. Next they'll be hitting the town, or their car will. The police are waiting for something to happen before they intervene. The two-year-old says whisky when they ask what he wants to drink. I hear they have a serious criminal record, a string of complaints and domestic accidents but they won't hand the kids over to social services. As for mine, he's reeling by now, made to balance on one leg and touch his nose with the opposite hand. They have him repeat Arabic words and laugh at his pronunciation, now words in Farsi, my son doesn't know any languages and they smack him over the head. Where was I taking him at that age. Why didn't

I teach him another language, when did he start to talk. We wait for him till closing time. Then the vase stands up with frozen feet and as they're throwing us out I say we're going to the boy sprawled with the others on the jetty. We're going I repeat, and my handbag springs open on its golden chain and everything falls out. And I never even touched my crème de cassis or glass of sparkling rosé. They help me gather my stuff, one tries on the lipstick, another scowls into the hand mirror, my papers blowing away, my menthol cigarettes rolling downhill, the silver lighter decorated with my photo. I'm taking him with me, sorry guys, sorry, and they all crack up, mocking my sorry guys sorry, mocking my outfit, kicking the mummy's boy, it seems I'm not looking my best.

I drive with my eyes shut. He plays at opening them with a toothpick. At flipping my eyelids inside out to turn them milky white. Why aren't I dead, Mum, like millions of other people. His teenage questions, his primordial turmoil. What did they give you to sniff. Don't talk as if you'd got used to living without me, you're right here and I'm telling you all about her, about your mum like I'm explaining who she is so you can get to know her better, so you can learn to love her from afar. All

I remember is that years ago a tall man came to collect me from school and I had no idea what had happened. He came over, asked if I was your son, took me to see you in a room and I still had no idea what was going on. Every one of us stumbles onto this path in the end he said and took me to a bar for a snack. I asked for a coffee and the taste of the bitter grains lingered, I didn't understand but then there were the times in that old Beetle with the sliding roof and piano music, me turning the dial and you turning it back and the entire afternoon going by.

Just outside his office, up on the hill, the first day of harvest season. We smoke roll-ups and he coughs and says he'll never be beautiful like me, he doesn't have my features. I stroke his curls, he's not a looker but his day will come. We have dog-ends between our fingers and tobacco sticking to our gums when we see him coming towards us. Me dolled up, him in his tuned car. I check myself over for signs of our malaria days. He steps forward as if to shield me from an oncoming wave and turns to face my son. Greets him, asks if he needs that summer job or not. Asks how old he'll be by the holidays, says he can start the next week if he's desperate. Tells him the hourly rate. My son bursts out laughing and he doesn't get the joke. He walks away after saying hi and looking me up and down. Wait, I haven't said anything yet, my son calls after him. I move away like someone trying not to get wet. I came to tell you you're my dad. He fails to react. We're a family now, the three of us, don't you recognise me? Can't you see we're the same? Together at last, Dad, time for the three of us to have some adventures. I see him turn pale. I'll have my parents spooning in bed on Sunday mornings, be able to use the plural, have double the fights. Stop talking nonsense, I say and thump him on the back. And the man lets out a breath. Just look at her. Look how beautiful my mother is this morning. Yes he says, compliant, looking at me, very beautiful. Just like old times, my son observes, you never got to see how she was back then but she still looks exactly the same. No one says a word. I need to go, I've got a meeting, a hellish day in store.

No, you can't go, she's come here to talk to you, take another good look at her, he says, forcing his head in my direction and leaving us alone. And I think he got scared. Don't use your son as an excuse, well then don't wash your hands of us. What's your son doing here anyway, this is between you and me. What did you bring him for. I didn't bring him, he just goes where I go. I had to replace all the windows, the skylights, hire security, take the dog to hospital, it cost a fortune. Now let me go in, I'll stop by and see you when I'm done. My eyes fill with tears. She's saying she wants to see you now, she's asking you for something and you're not even listening. And when he doesn't respond my son runs at him, head-butting him in the stomach. I watch them crash through the vines, roll this way and that, stab at each other with stakes and then toss them aside. I catch glimpses of thighs, glimpses of wrists. They get up but then they're tumbling on through the planted fields, groping for some hedge clippers, I see shoulders flip over and snap with the thorns. My son wins thanks to his karate. He only lets him crawl to safety after agreeing to a date at the end of the day. He's covered in cuts. I wait outside while they go in for cold compresses and a wash. The delinquents wave from their motorbikes and leave a black trail of benzine in the air.

I suggest a boat trip, a peaceful reconciliation, an ending weaving around the islands on the far side. A visit to the sandy cays by the riverbank overlooking the tennis courts and tourist camps, bungalows and imitation allotments. I wait for him, we make our way down on foot and take the path to the last wild river. Going somewhere else so no one will see us, he's all in favour. My son leaves us to it, I glance back and have the feeling he's following, dawdling behind, but I'm not sure and cast him out of my thoughts. At the water's edge, the banks of heavy sand and boats with yellow moorings in an uneven line. He takes my hand and we clamber down, waltz into the hut like a couple of tourists, hire a boat under a false name and I insist on two sets of oars. No one's looking, relax I tell him when we kiss for the first time. No one ever comes out here. We follow the gentle river past dikes, marshes, reservoirs, isn't it glorious I say but he doesn't buy it. It's all so glorious I say, this river is sacred and his eyes cloud over. You won't have an answer, but for argument's sake, how often do you think about me? How often would you say I pass before you like a veil, a blanket, a gust of wind? Do you see me when you're falling asleep? How obsessed are you with me, like for instance right now you're there in the blue of the sky. I see you in the oar as it swings, in the spray from the geyser, and when I stagger to the fridge not knowing what else to drink or where I even am, there you are on the rusty shelf, at the bottom of the bottle. We're both rowing, at opposite ends of the boat. Life elapsing a little at a time. I look at him and it's a heart attack, an outer shell crushing my jaw and aorta, a prickling all over, an imminent fall. Ingesting an animal, the flesh sliding stiff down my gullet, a faltering pulse, a migraine. We rowed on and I could have sworn that a low, sweet melody was playing beneath us, down on the riverbed among currents and reefs, among sardines, jack mackerel, sea bass. Look what I brought, and I produce fruit, coloured juices and bread for us both. We could have a picnic on one of these little islands. But that wasn't it, not even close, more like suck on my fingers, gnaw on my arms, chew me up and turn it all to oblivion. You know what I was thinking the first time I saw you, I don't know if you saw me then, did you? That first time, I remember, you were standing tall on the hill. You looked like a chieftain, a rugged high commissioner, a paramilitary boss, shielding your eyes. And you know what I said to myself when I slammed on the brakes halfway to where I was going? If I have to rape him, I'll rape him. And he's looking at me God knows how. And it's all so idyllic. Do you see the car with its lights off in the middle of the road, just before the bend? Do you see that car with its lights off right in the middle, being dodged at sixty miles per hour? I was risking my life from the outset. No,

I didn't, I didn't see a car stop, I remember some lips the colour of my grapes that went by time and again as I was planting the vines. Again and again with those nectar lips, how many times did you come? When I'm clinging onto the last of my life, there'll be a single true moment of happiness.

That's a cat jumping out over there. An aquatic cat, it reminds me of mine, I think it's chasing the same destiny. What do you mean, what cat, what are you on about now. A ghost. See, this is when you scare me, saying things like that. How about this island. Or that one there, over behind the breakwater. I don't know. How could I possibly scare you, look at me, one kick and I'd go flying. I don't know, but sometimes you do. I've always wanted to go there, cosy warm feet, make a fire, explore, huddle up in a tent. And I row, aiming for the furthest islands. Against his will. You're going too far and he corrects our course, rowing the other way. And I row even harder, hauling the canoe but he doesn't give in and it's a nautical battle until I straddle him, fondle him, make his head spin. How do you feel now? Fine, he says, better, much better in fact, you men need that to loosen up, right, lucky it's there for you. Look at this immaculate sky. We'll leave the rest to the water now, let it take as long as the whims of the tide. And the water does my bidding, draws the boat towards the island. When we strike, our eyes are closed against the heat. I finish the job on my own. Better find some muscles, looks like I'll need them. I manoeuvre the boat, bring it to a stop and stand up, making it quiver. Then an athletic leap in my heels and I moor it. He stays put. I walk around our island. Everything peaceful, virginal. It's the best one of all, I yell gathering pine cones, shamrocks and bright green flowers, skipping in my dress through black vegetable snares, there are dragonfruits, jackfruits, starfruits, purple plantains and prickly pears, you're going to love it. There's a lake, maybe we can go for a swim and get guzzled by the whirlpool. Look at those plants, the way they branch into bushes, steadfast in this shifting terrain. I crouch down and sink to my waist in the swamp, see the roots suffocating deep down. But I keep one eye on him so he doesn't row away, let him stay lost in thought on that tightly-bound boat.

I would have made a good junkie, or maybe a beatnik, if it weren't for the fact I'm from a fancy family, worlds from the gutter, with a mum and dad who spoke at mealtimes and even looked at each other. If it weren't for the fact they stroked the pets and praised their daughter's beauty. The beauty of youth which leaves you no choice, people want it and you have to let it go. You can't not dress up, you can't hide in the shadows, have you ever met a goddess who works in a basement? It's impossible, it wouldn't be allowed. But then the flipside, when they let you go after twenty years and you have to find work stacking shelves or selling spare parts. Still, look at you, you're not selling anything, you're free. And he fell silent. An improvement. I'd have made a good mud wrestler, a good hunter, a lucha libre contender, waking up every day and getting my teeth into something, it must be fascinating living to destroy. But as for you, you plant, water, sow, harvest, always productive. A useful man, and I was a useful woman. How many times can a person shine, once, twice, we're shining on this island. Shall we look for some coconuts? Anything could grow here. We'll crack them open on the tree trunks and let the clear juice stream down our throats. And then a writhing embrace on the crest of the hill. You're my youth, my reverberation. And we're rolling around, faster and faster, and nothing can account for the suddenness and none of it feels like the end, his hands more expressive than the river. He looks at his watch. I look at the half-moon sliding into view and beside it Neptune or Venus ablaze. Is it Venus? I didn't know planets could scatter golden pollen. I need to go, it's getting dark. A spring night but he's checking the time. Don't keep checking the time, don't do anything, don't insult me, I want us to wait for the dawn cloaked in desiccated seaweed, I bet it'll be magnificent. You never listen to what I'm saying, you go on about the sunrise but I have to get back, we're, where even are we, somewhere, I can't see a thing, this is dangerous. On the islands opposite, what do you mean dangerous, we just need to go back across. And how are we meant to go back across if we can't see our way through the current? See what, see why? You never accept anything, you can't accept anything, hence the hospital and all those seizures. I need to get back right away, it's crucial, you're not listening. The swamp beast stands and shakes himself off. Plus I have no signal, people will be wondering where I am, I have responsibilities, dependents, a life. Some nights don't smell of anything and I think this will be one, an entirely odourless night. I'd relax if I were you, we'll build a fire, I've brought some food. We'll keep warm, bed down on patches of soft earth and tomorrow we'll go back. Then he lost it, fell silent and wouldn't even look at me. I have no signal, he says. You're being cruel, you can't just

71

say you have no signal and he went to unmoor the boat. I watched serene as he undid the knot I'd tied with all my might, as he pulled the boat towards him and one oar tumbled over the side. The light was fading too fast, everything going my way but he still had time to slip through my fingers.

What are you doing I said in a voice like a threat. What exactly are you doing, what the hell do you think you're doing I barked and had to get to my feet. Such a shame to dismantle the moment, to have to leave the warm sand, turn my gaze from the moonrise. I jumped onto his back but he shook me off. I climbed back on and held tighter but he threw me to the ground. Something hit me as I fell. He got into the boat but I sprang in behind and bit him on the wrist. Another oar slithered into the water, to be devoured by the carnivorous plants. I'm asking you to come back for one minute, that's all, and we'll talk. Put yourself in my place for just one second, I need to get out of here. What place is that exactly and why don't you put yourself in mine, now we've finally reached perfection, this is our last chance. What perfection, what are you on about, this is making no sense, you're unhinged. I came here, I did what you wanted, end of story. Sure, unhinged. What? But all that was impossible, the questions, the two voices. I don't know how he could bring himself to get out of there, my body was aching all over and I lay down. A ridiculous sight, lolling like a film star on a nudist beach, like a femme who thinks she's fatale. No, no. We just need to go and find something to drink, tell ourselves we're young and living the life. And there was a silence, we burst out laughing, my knee on his Adam's apple until we heard a noise, we weren't alone, the boat drifting away or an alligator under the surface. I straddled him, accelerating everything. And he penetrated me with more hunger than I knew existed, possession not this way or that not desire not two bodies not sex but something beyond thought. Not a man but all of him all at once like the ultimate dream. Then the noise again and he wants to go and see. I don't let him, I reel him back in, but he wants to find out what's making that racket, what's shrieking in the distance. I make him stay, he throws a punch and my bone shifts under my skin. I didn't mean to, he says. I stare at him, deformed, drooling but smiling, passive now and waiting for the end. I say goodbye but he's there in the blood on my face. I wriggle my buried toes and hit him back. I could rip you limb from fucking limb I say and that's when I thought I saw my son jump into the river. Arms thrashing all around in a fizzing frenzy, he was swimming towards us and sending out great jets of water. He tries to meet him halfway, signalling, here, over here, but my son's clumsy flailing buys us time and he's still on the other side. Thank God I never took him to swimming lessons. Please don't let him get here, let the tide beat him, let the river hold him back. I might be stupid but even I can see my son's clamouring for my return, his mouth full of water, coming to my rescue with his big brawny arms. That's if he's even my son, I'm suddenly not sure, how could I ever have conceived him. I stand and watch as he swims frantically on, sometimes floundering underwater, in thrall to the current, swimming and calling me, struggling to the surface, floating on his back and gulping for air. He's still there like a log being swept along, the river bringing him closer but what does it matter while this hell of desire doesn't stop. I throw myself at him again and again, kiss him with my dislocated jaw, disgusting I think he says. He pulls my hair, I pull his, we don't let go and white-knuckled climb higher and pull and pull and pull until we collapse into the sand. That didn't go well, it's all over, he says, the die is cast and there's nothing we can do. And I kiss him once more, as hard as I can but he recoils and I feel him take a breath. Then a crash and then the echo. The last ray of sun kind of spins, kind of skips and ricochets off the bushes, the sky glimmers on the water and everything's a miracle again. So this is loving, I say to myself, and he leans in and rips off my head.

CHARCO PRESS

Director & Editor: Carolina Orloff
Director: Samuel McDowell

www.charcopress.com

Tender was published on
90gsm Munken Premium Cream paper.

The text was designed using Bembo 11.5 and ITC Galliard.

Printed in October 2021 by TJ Books
Padstow, Cornwall, PL28 8RW using responsibly
sourced paper and environmentally-friendly adhesive.